WHAT THE GOOD MAN DOES IS ALWAYS RIGHT

HANS CHRISTIAN ANDERSEN'S
WHAT THE GOOD MAN DOES IS ALWAYS RIGHT

Pictures by RICK SCHREITER

The Dial Press, Inc.
New York

"Let us begin..."

I take it for granted that you have been in the country and seen a very old farmhouse with a thatched roof, with mosses and small plants growing wide upon the thatch. There is a stork's nest on the summit of the gable, for we can't do without the stork. The walls of the house are sloping and the windows are low, and only one of the latter is made so that it will open. The baking oven sticks out of the wall like a little fat

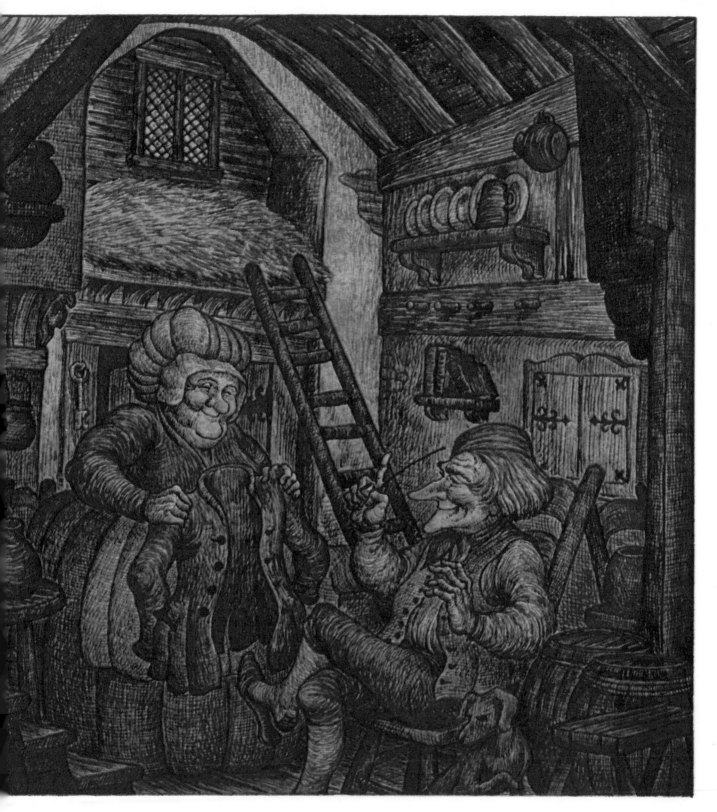

body. The elder tree hangs over the eaves, and beneath its branches, at the foot of the fence, is a pool of water in which a few ducks are enjoying themselves. There is a dog, too, who barks at all comers.

Just such a farmhouse stood out in the country, and in this house dwelled an old couple, a peasant and his wife. Small as was their property, there was one article among it that they could do without—a horse,

which lived on the grass it found by the side of the highway. The old peasant rode into the town on this horse, and often his neighbors borrowed it of him and rendered the old couple some service in return for the loan of it. But they thought it would be best if they sold the horse or exchanged it for something that might be more useful to them. But what might this *something* be?

"You'll know that best, old man," said the wife. "It is fair day today, so ride into town and get rid of the horse for money, or make a good exchange. Whichever you do will be right to me. Ride off to the fair."

And she fastened his neckerchief for him, for she could do that better than he could. Then she brushed his hat around and around with the palm of her hand and gave him a kiss. So he rode away upon the horse

that was to be sold or to be bartered for something else. Yes, the good man knew what he was about.

The sun shone hotly down and not a cloud was to be seen in the sky. The road was very dusty, for many people, who were all bound for the fair, were driving or riding or walking upon it. There was no shelter anywhere.

Among the rest, a man was trudging along and driving a cow to the fair. The cow was as beautiful a creature as any cow can be.

"She gives good milk, I'm sure," said the peasant. "That would be a very good exchange—the cow for the horse."

"Hello, you there with the cow!" he said. "I tell you what: I fancy a horse costs more than a cow, but I don't care for that. A cow would be

more useful to me. If you like, we'll exchange."

"To be sure I will," said the man, and they exchanged accordingly.

So that was settled and the peasant might have turned back, for he had done the business he came to do. But as he had once made up his mind to go to the fair, he determined to go on, merely to have a look at it. And so he went on to the town with his cow.

Leading the animal, he strode sturdily on, and after a short time he overtook a man who was driving a sheep. It was a good fat sheep, with a fine fleece on its back.

"I should like to have that fellow," said our peasant. "He would find plenty of grass by our fence, and in the winter we could keep him in the room with us. Perhaps it would be more practical to have a sheep

instead of a cow. Shall we exchange?"

The man with the sheep was quite ready and the bargain was struck.
So our peasant went along on the highway with his sheep.

Soon he overtook another man, who came into the road from a field,
carrying a great goose under his arm.

"That's a heavy thing you have there. It has plenty of feathers and

plenty of fat, and would look well tied to a string and paddling in the water at our place. That would be something for my good woman. She could make all kinds of profit out of it. How often she has said, 'If we only had a goose!' Now perhaps she can have one, and if possible it shall be hers. Shall we exchange? I'll give you my sheep for your goose and thank you into the bargain.''

The other man had not the least objection. And accordingly they exchanged, and our peasant became the proprietor of the goose.

By this time he was very near the town. The crowd on the highroad became greater and greater. There was quite a crush of men and cattle. They walked in the road, close by the fence, and at the toll booth they even walked into the tollman's potato field, where his own fowl was

strutting about with a string tied to its leg, lest it take fright at the crowd and stray away and so be lost. This fowl had short tail feathers and winked with both its eyes and looked very cunning. "Cluck, cluck!" said the fowl.

What it thought when it said this I cannot tell you, but directly our good man saw it, he thought, "That's the finest fowl I've ever seen in

my life! Why, it's finer than our parson's finest hen. On my word, I should like to have that fowl. A fowl can always find a grain or two and can almost keep itself. I think it would be a good exchange if I could get that for my goose."

"Shall we exchange?" he asked the toll taker.

"Exchange?" repeated the man. "Well, that would not be a bad thing."

And so they exchanged. The toll taker at the booth kept the goose, and the peasant carried away the fowl.

Now he had done a good deal of business on his way to the fair, and he was hot and tired. He wanted something to eat and a glass of brandy to drink, and soon he was in front of the inn. He was just about to step in when the hostler came out, so they met at the door. The

hostler was carrying a sack.

"What have you in that sack?" asked the peasant.

"Rotten apples," answered the hostler. "A whole sackful of them—enough to feed the pigs with."

"Why, that's a terrible waste! I should like to take them to my good woman at home. Last year the old tree bore only a single apple, and we

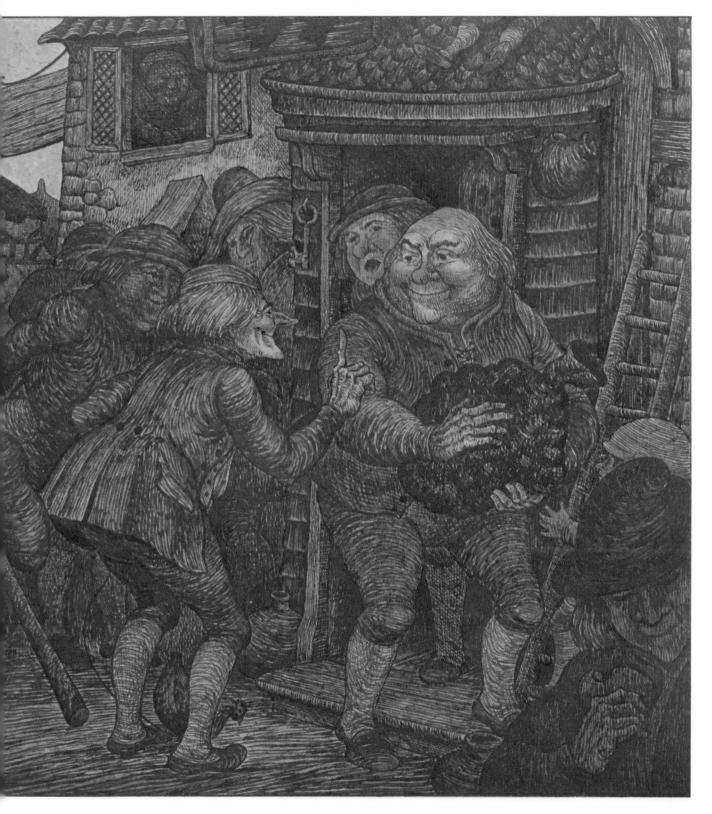

kept it in the cupboard till it was quite rotten and spoiled. But if I take your apples, my woman shall have a whole sackful! Yes, I shall be glad to show them to her.''

"What will you give me for the sackful?" asked the hostler.

"What will I give? I will give my fowl in exchange," replied the peasant.

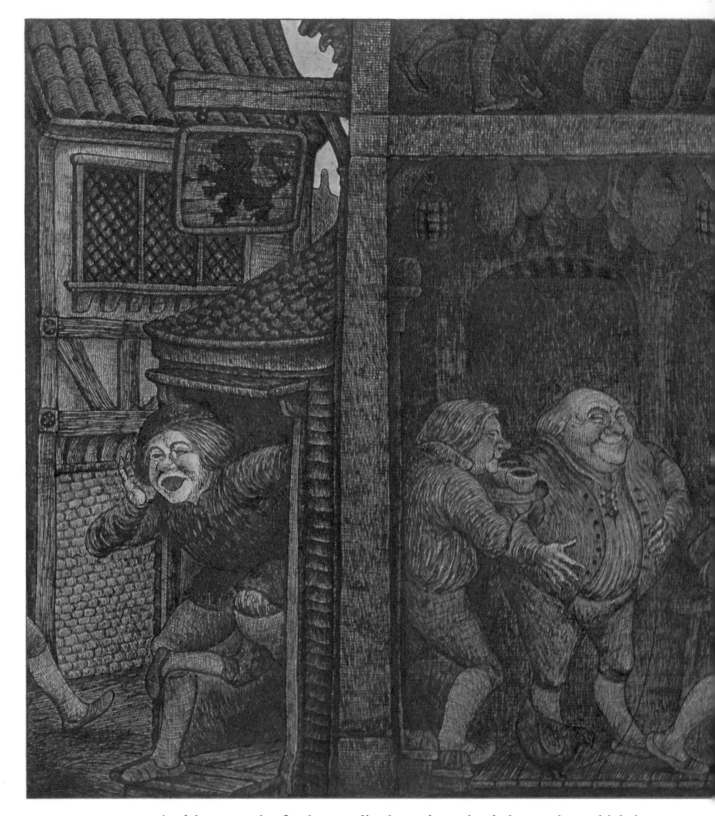

And he gave the fowl accordingly and received the apples, which he carried into the dining room. He leaned the sack carefully by the stove, and then went to the table. But the stove was hot: he had not thought of that. Many guests were present—horse dealers, oxherds, and two Englishmen. And the two Englishmen were so rich that their pockets bulged out with gold coins until they almost burst.

Hiss-s-s! hiss-s-s! What was that by the stove? The apples were beginning to roast!

"What is that?"

"Why, do you know—" said our peasant.

And he told the whole story of the horse he had changed for a cow, and all the rest of it, down to the apples.

"Well, your old woman will give it to you well when you get home!"
said one of the two Englishmen. "There will be a disturbance."

"What? Give me what?" said the peasant. "She will kiss me and say,
'What the good man does is always right.'"

"Shall we wager?" said the Englishman. "We'll wager coined gold
by the ton—a hundred pounds and as much more as you can carry."

"A bushel will be enough," replied the peasant. "I can only set the bushel of apples against it, and I'll throw myself and my good woman into the bargain. I can't do better than that."

"Done! Taken!"

And the bet was made. The innkeeper's carriage came up, and the Englishmen got in and the peasant got in.

Away they went, and soon they stopped before the peasant's farm.

"Good evening, old woman."

"Good evening, old man."

"I've made the exchange."

"Yes, you understand what you're about," said the woman. And she embraced him and paid no attention to the strange guests, nor did she

notice the sack.

"I got a cow in exchange for the horse," said he.

"Heaven be thanked!" said she. "What glorious milk we shall now have, and butter and cheese on the table. That was a most capital exchange!"

"Yes, but I changed the cow for a sheep."

"Ah, that's better still!" cried the wife. "You always think of everything. We have just pasture enough for a sheep. Ewe's milk and cheese, and woolen jackets and stockings! The cow cannot give those, and her hairs will only come off. How you think of everything!"

"But I changed away the sheep for a goose."

"Then this year we shall really have roast goose to eat, my dear old

man. You are always thinking of something to give me pleasure. How charming that is! We can let the goose walk about with a string tied to her leg, and she'll grow fatter still before we roast her."

"But I gave away the goose for a fowl," said the man.

"A fowl? That *was* a good exchange!" replied the woman. "The fowl will lay eggs and hatch them, and we shall have chickens. We shall have

a whole poultry yard! Oh, that's just what I was wishing for. You could not have made a better choice."

"Yes, but I exchanged the fowl for a sack of shriveled apples."

"What! I must positively kiss you for that!" exclaimed the wife. "My dear good husband! Now I'll tell you something. Do you know, you had hardly left me this morning before I began thinking how I could

give you something very nice this evening. I thought it should be pan-
cakes with savory herbs. I had eggs, and bacon too. But I lacked herbs.
So I went over to the schoolmaster's, as they have herbs there, I know.
But the schoolmistress is a mean woman, though she looks so sweet. I
begged her to lend me a handful of herbs.

" 'Lend!' she answered me, 'nothing at all grows in our garden, not

even a shriveled apple. I could not even lend you a shriveled apple, my dear woman.' But now *I* can lend *her* ten, or a whole sackful. That I'm very glad of. That makes me laugh." And with that she gave him another resounding kiss.

"I like that!" exclaimed both the Englishmen together. "Always going downhill, and always merry! That's worth the money!" So they

paid a hundred pounds of gold to the peasant, who was not scolded
but kissed.

The End.